# The Tale of Rescue

# The Tale of Rescue

## MICHAEL J. ROSEN

### ILLUSTRATED BY STAN FELLOWS

CANDLEWICK PRESS

Text copyright © 2015 by Michael J. Rosen
Illustrations copyright © 2015 by Stan Fellows

First edition 2015

Library of Congress Catalog Card Number 2014949722
ISBN 978-0-7636-7167-9

15 16 17 18 19 20 CCP 10 9 8 7 6 5 4 3 2 1

Printed in Shenzhen, Guangdong, China

This book was typeset in Centaur MT.
The illustrations were done in watercolor.

Candlewick Press
99 Dover Street
Somerville, Massachusetts 02144

visit us at www.candlewick.com

*I would say that this story is inspired by and dedicated
to my own dog, Chant, an Australian cattle dog, a rescue —
but that small honor needs to be extended to all the animal companions
who rescue each of us from the lives we imagine that we lead.*

M. R.

# Chapter One

This is a tale about a cattle dog. She had a name, but only one person knew it and usually he called her with herding words like *cast* and *wait* and *bye* and *that'll do*. Mostly he called her with whistles.

This heeler had been born in the farmer's barn. She had lived there, with an always changing herd of cattle, her entire life. As had her mother. As had her mother's sire. Each and every cow knew the black-ticked cattle dog by her stares and by her barks—the high-pitched yelps that signaled an intruder; the whining yodel of excitement when the farmer appeared; the grumble-huff that meant "pay attention" or "freeze"; the staccato woofs that forced them to retreat or split apart; the muffled yips as her paws flicked in a dream. They knew the rake and jab of her nails against their hides, the pinch and grip of her teeth nipping their heels to get them moving. (Yes, that's why cattle dogs are also known as heelers.)

Bred with the stamina to work for hours—maneuvering a large herd, a cattle dog might run seventy-five miles in a day—she lived for the hours spent with the farmer.

*Cast!* She gathered up the cattle.

*Bye!* She veered around left of the herd.

*Away!* She flew around right.

*Look back!* She instantly halted, pivoted, and dashed in the opposite direction to locate a missing animal.

At dawn and at dusk, she focused all her attention and funneled all her energy into marching the cattle from pasture to pasture, from barn to corral. Although the cattle dog weighed fifty pounds and each of her forty cows weighed more than a thousand, there was never a question of who was in charge. The heeler directed, stopped, separated, and gathered more than 40,000 pounds of cattle with barks, stares, nips, and a swiftness and agility that allowed her to charge among the herd's 160 legs, weave under their bellies — under their milk-heavy udders — and even clamber onto

their bony backs. It was not easy work, but it was the work her kind had been bred to do. It was the work she loved.

This is also a tale about a mother, a father, and their ten-year-old son. They, too, had names, of course, but no one else in this story knew them.

A family from Florida, they had rented a cabin in the foothills of the Appalachian Mountains. When the mother had lived in Ohio, nearby cousins had booked the cabins at this lodge one year and celebrated New Year's Eve there. While both parents had grown up in the Midwest, their son had never experienced a winter with snow. The lodge had recently been renovated, according to friends, so it sounded like the ideal choice. Indeed, upon arrival, their timing seemed perfect: sunshine, mild temperatures, and light flurries to freshen the full foot of snow that already carpeted the countryside. One nearby field—a distinctly defined rectangle—was polka-dotted with bits of dried cornstalks poking through the white. Otherwise, as far as the horizons, the snowy ground was untrammeled: not a footprint, not a tire track—and certainly none of the gray slush and spattered mud that bordered the weaving roads that conducted them to the lodge.

The family rented cross-country skis and partly glided, partly stomped, across the landscape; their overlapping parallel tracks left an empty musical staff on the blank pages of the smooth fields. Later, they returned on foot and their boot prints added the notes.

They built a family of snowmen — father, mother, son — exactly their heights! They borrowed sleds from the lodge; they joined a bonfire and roasted hot dogs; they stockpiled a mound of snowballs and waged a midnight snowball fight. The paired hearts of deer tracks stamped in the snow, stalactites of icicles along their cabin's timber eaves, snow angels, frost-crazed windowpanes — their snapshots captured every wintery thing they'd never encountered in Florida.

On their last vacation morning, a blanket of thick, wet snowflakes had settled on everything while they'd slept. The snow spackled the evergreens' boughs. The snow whitewashed

the porch chairs and the picnic table. It even erased the telephone wires. Only hints of color peeked through: a yield sign's yellow, their car roof's blue. Another few inches had piled onto the foot or so of snow through which they'd been tromping. Out the cabin's windows, the ground glistened like finely grated dia-monds—the sand at the beach near their home did the same thing—when the sun pried a hole in the cloud cover.

Before breakfast, the family decided to hike the half-mile to the lodge. But no sooner had they bundled into their parkas, scarves, boots, and gloves, than the sky disappeared. Tilting back their heads and gazing straight up: a dense, strangely beautiful confetti of snow

blocked everything but itself from view. A sudden gust whooshed the flakes sideways for a few seconds, and then, just as abruptly, as if it had second thoughts, allowed the snow to stream downward again.

In Florida, in years past, the family had witnessed raging tides and relentless storms and thrashing hurricanes, but nothing like this snow's dramatic antics. They had never experienced a whiteout.

# Chapter Two

Ten minutes later, the family had nearly reached the lodge, although the squall of snow prevented them from seeing it. White insisted on being the only detail within sight; snow, the only destination. So they turned around, fit their boots backward into their steps, and retreated toward their cabin.

Their previous tracks grew shallower and shallower as they trudged onward; too soon, their old steps were buried in new snow. The family wasn't lost—but nothing offered them a clue of where they might be heading.

Two more inches of snow fell in the next half hour. Strong winds had mounded drifts deeper than the boy's waist. His father carried him as long as he could. But slogging through such deep snow with his son's additional weight, he was soon out of breath.

Only a bird soaring above them—and no birds appeared to be flying in the storm—could adequately appreciate the route they had traveled: They had zigzagged. They had circled. They weren't lost—they knew they had to be close to either the lodge or the cabin. Yet, as if they were trapped in a snow globe, they had

come no closer to either dwelling; they were stuck in the very same place as the storm's flurries swirled around them and around them.

If only they *had* been in a snow globe where the same snowy scene simply repeats. The weather in their dome of heaven worsened. Remember, the family hadn't eaten. Fatigue had overtaken them. The snow had so deepened that no one could lift a boot high enough to step out of and over the snow in order to place the next step. They could only shuffle forward, parting the snow with their boots, knees, and waists.

And they were, all three of them, scared—and, of course, freezing cold. When the wind kicked up, the parents sandwiched their son between them and stared into each other's eyes to see if the other thought there was any chance that everything would be all right.

Was it an hour? Two hours? Relentlessly, the squall dumped its wet snow. Now the accumulation of the previous snows, the earlier wet blanket, and the slushy flakes was deep as the parents' waists. The family plodded ahead, single file: The father shoved and tromped the snow to make the passage easier for his wife; she did the same for their son. The wind's blasts slapped their faces; every tear and bead of sweat burned their skin. They had to squint so that the snowflakes would melt on their lashes instead of stab at their eyes.

Father, mother, son — the idea of screaming for help crossed each of their minds. But they all realized the wind's howling would drown out anything they called. Besides, who was around to hear? Besides, who wanted to unwrap and rewrap a scarf in this biting wind, even for the brief moment it would take to scream? Still, the father did shape his lips and tongue to whistle like a siren. Two and three times, his piercing wail rang in their ears.

Did another hour pass? Two hours? By the time the blizzard weakened or simply shifted its intensity to another county, four feet of snow surrounded the family. Lifting the heels of his boots, the boy could just see above the snow.

Drifts arched well over his head. While nightfall was still hours away, even if they mustered yet another burst of will and energy, they had no landmark to orient their course. If they'd held a map of this, it would show no north, no roads, no cities. They were lost, even if they were not so far from shelter.

Although the parents had no clue what to do, their son's face told them they had to think of something. Together, they stomped in a tight circle, trampling a depression in the snow that was wide enough for the three of them to evade the wind. They hunkered together in that den, squished together, a circle of thighs packed as tight as orange segments.

It was warmer there. No one had to shout

to be heard, although no one could think of much to say, let alone of what to do next. Every now and again, the father struggled to a standing position and whistled. And whistled.

When the snow changed to freezing rain, the first droplets pinged as they struck the snow. But quickly, a drenching rain fell, seeping into the snow and compacting it. Eventually, a glaze of ice coated the ground. It quickened into a thin shell that even crowned the family's hoods and their shoulders. Then a hard crust formed; punched with a gloved fist, silver cracks shattered the lip of the icy bowl in which the family crouched.

# Chapter Three

Remember, this is also a tale about a cattle dog. From the moment the squall descended and the farmer called, the dog had been driving cows from their placid, all-morning meal at the round hay bales to the corral that connected the nearest pasture to the barn. She had coaxed the eight new calves inside the barn. She had discovered a cow, almost ready to calve, who'd sequestered herself beneath a thicket of blackberry canes by the frozen stream, and brought her back to the yard. Deep snow made the heeler's demanding work all the more tiring; she was curled on the seat of the tractor parked below the hayloft when the faint thread of a whistle pierced her sleep.

The dog scampered to her feet and jumped from the tractor's cab. The whistle — it definitely was not one of the farmer's commands. Pointed in the feeble sound's direction, her tall ears waited for the whistle to repeat. Stockstill, she listened. . . . Nothing. Nothing but the rooster fluttering his wings for no good reason. Nothing but a cow pie splatting on the barnfloor muck. Nothing — *something!* She bolted from the barn, hurdled a wheelbarrow, the rooster, and everything else the happenstance of cows forced her to encounter, scrabbled to the top rail of the steel-tube fence, vaulted out—all four legs fully extended—and raced across the snow.

*Raced* would have been the right word if the field were anything but four feet of compacted snow capped with ice. A heeler's legs, remember, are twelve inches long; the snow was four times that . . . in its lowest spots. Even the dog's nose reached no higher than thirty inches when she craned to sniff. This time, *racing* meant smacking hard into the crusted snow and slipping—one foot punching through the shell of ice, stumbling, and scrambling to get

both feet repositioned. *Racing* meant firing up all the power and quickness and determination that she'd been exercising all her life with her cattle: She pounced onto the ice as if it were a cow's back. She twisted, then righted herself, as if a cow's hoof had tripped her. She struggled forward and onward, springing up and onto the snow, sinking down, and leaping again, ignoring the exhaustion and pain, because everything, absolutely everything depended on her. As it always did.

Finally, the whistle repeated. The towers of her pricked-up ears captured the vibration. At the same instant, as if the sound had a scent as well, her nose inhaled something foreign. Not the pungency of a calf's afterbirth. Not a coyote's musk or the rotted squirrel it had killed. Not anything like the grease and orange of the farmer's hands or his sweaty, talcum-powdered boots. The heeler heaved herself again and again onto the blockade of snow, her nose alone directing her across the snow-emptied acres.

When the father rose again to whistle, he thought he noticed something in the distance that wasn't white. Small, dark — it disappeared. It reappeared — was the wind cartwheeling a broken umbrella? A luffing plastic grocery bag? It disappeared. He hunkered down again with his wife and son.

But not long after that, all three cocked their heads at a noise that clearly wasn't rain. It clearly wasn't wind. They held still, listening harder. Something crackled in the snow. *Punch-crunch.* Something scraped the ice. Whatever made those sounds grew closer.

When the heeler saw two faces peer above the ice, she let out a sharp, excited bark that would have alarmed her entire herd. The faces instantly withdrew — fast as moles retreat when the dog detects their slightest movement under the leaves before she pounces. Then she produced a string of howling barks that the drizzle's static muffled. She lurched forward again and again, the pitch of her barks even more urgent. No matter that her energy was depleted from the ordeal of her journey, she continued to crouch and jump, trying to rouse these stragglers.

In their shallow bunker, the family ducked their heads and linked arms. They formed a fortress of coats. The cattle dog's barks clapped above them as if the skies had added thunder to its theme of disaster. They gritted their teeth and squeezed their parched lips together. Even the boy's sobbing turned silent. How could they be trapped in a snowstorm—*and* attacked by some savage dog?

But then the barking modulated to a whine and the heeler leaned, then slid, into the shallow den. She prodded her muzzle between the hoods of their parkas. She slithered behind the father's sloped back. She clawed at their arms, linked together. With her front paws pulling and her back paws pushing, she wedged her nose, then her head and shoulders, and then the whole of her body into the space she had prized among their locked-together arms and legs. And she lay there, wedged below their shallow, bitter breaths, panting and listening.

Chapter Four

There are moments when the exceptional human power of speech fails, when silence is called upon to carry whatever needs to be said. That silence — with a few sounds like barks and whistles — serves most every other creature.

So it was that the parents could not think of what to say to each other, of what to tell their son, of what to command or beg of the dog whose chest heaved so rapidly among them. The boy rested his cheek on the dog's chilled and soaked coat. When a tear spilled across his cheek, its warmth surprised him—the furnace inside him could still heat the water in his eyes. A second later, it cooled on the dog's cold fur. But as he held his face against her silver-black coat, her body's heat rose and eased the frost's rawness on that patch of his skin.

He placed the other side of his face on the dog. He tugged the mittens from his numb fingers and slid his hands under the dog's belly. Once his own flesh thawed the clumps of ice that clung to her fur, the dog's heat radiated into his palms.

Soon, six cold hands flattened beneath

the cattle dog's body. What a wan furnace the four creatures built with their bodies' heat. Their exhales, the sudden touch of a chin, made the dog's ears twitch as they gathered words that were not *bye*, or *way*, or *that'll do*.

If only to force their minds away from what was happening — or what *might* happen — the family trained their attention on the dog. They had never encountered a cattle dog, to say nothing of cradling one within their arms and legs or of inhaling the odors of hay and manure and whatever else infused her sodden coat.

The boy gripped her front paw in his hand — it was remarkably small. Even though she had come to them across how many acres or miles of ice, even though their bodies had no real heat to offer her, the paw seemed to hold even more heat than her body. She flexed her black toenails in his palm; he could sense the power of her forearms' muscles. A thin stream of blood seeped from her dewclaw onto the boy's lap.

The mother made long strokes with her numb hands down the dog's coat; the silver-white ticking gleamed even in the limited light. The tips of her fingers wriggled into the soft, felt-like undercoat. She pointed out the tail — there was but a nub of a tail — to her husband and son. The hind legs were feathered with light hair, she remarked, almost like a white-tailed deer.

The father cradled the dog's head, smoothing the fur on her ears that folded back against her head at his touch. He gazed into her round, brown eyes: Unlike any dog he had ever known, she returned his gaze and didn't look away.

After a long time, which was still shy of long enough, the dog scooted backward, retreating from the family's embrace. As the heeler clawed and climbed to the surface, someone surely wished, *If we only had paper to write a note.* One of the three surely thought, *Is there anything we can tie to its collar?* Someone surely said a prayer or asked for a miracle. They all wished the dog would stay.

The boy reached up and grabbed for one of the dog's rear paws. She spun around, fast as a cyclone, nipped his thumb, and without a moment's pause, continued that spin until she was racing again in the direction from which she had come.

*Nip* is the right word. The dog's teeth didn't break the boy's skin. It was a warning. It probably wouldn't have hurt at all had the boy's fingers not been tingling — frozen stiff and bloodless — from the hours of cold.

*Racing*, on the other hand, is even less the right word this time: The ice had thickened during the time the cattle dog had stayed with the family. Some leaps landed her on such unyielding ground that she skidded, paws splaying to each side. Other leaps, her body smashed the ice and she toppled forward; thin shards jabbed her. Her four limbs felt as if they had conflicting commands to obey, even as she had but one goal, but one place she had to be right then. No — sooner than then.

The father squinted to follow the only dark object in their world as it shrank and then, all of a sudden, vanished. He had seen a magician when he was his son's age: a white dove, a white handkerchief carefully draped over it — and instantly, nothing! Nothing but a crumpled cloth and applause. And the dove? Where was it?

And there they were, in this Ohio blizzard, left with nothing but an immeasurable white handkerchief.

Was this their best chance? The father played out another scenario: He could leave his wife and son to follow the dog's tracks while they were still visible. They had to lead some-where. She was no homeless animal. But how far she had traveled? And did he have some untapped endurance that could fuel him to wherever the dog lived? Yet even that assumed she headed there directly. And that people would be home. And that those people would be willing to *do* something. That was not their best chance. That was not a chance at all.

The wind had tapered off and the rain had ceased — for the moment. The dog's warmth lingered, but it was like a held breath . . . soon to expire. As nightfall approached, the fam-ily knew temperatures would plummet. They shared the quiet, in lieu of hope.

## Chapter Five

The cattle dog's impatient barks summoned the farmer from his bedroom. She saw his scowling face, his squinting eyes, when he yanked aside the curtain. Until that moment, she had always called the farmer from the barn, the pasture, or the corral when she needed him. But she had no coyote to report, no cow straining with a life-or-death birth. Now she waited five feet from his window, all but her head sunk beneath the snow.

By the time the farmer dressed, pulled on his boots, and unlocked the back door, the heeler had stationed herself beside the corral gate. She couldn't race up and back, up and back, as usual, to hurry the farmer to follow, so she barked and barked even as the farmer called, "That'll do!" She watched his flashlight beam survey the empty fields.

The farmer plodded too slowly through his backyard, but the cattle dog couldn't run her circles around him to convince him of the urgency. She couldn't dash forward and expect him to follow or leap into the farm cart as usual. He flipped on the dim barn lights. Nothing was wrong with the herd, but she couldn't deter the man from wasting time, pointing his bright circle on the ear tags of

every cow and calf—even the two roosters, even one of the barn cats.

On the floor of the dry barn, she regained her gait and her ability to better express her agitation. She coaxed the farmer to the far side of the barn and bounded, as much as she could, for a third time, into the path she had taken to and from the stranded people. The beam of the farmer's flashlight followed her—it traveled into the distance where she headed, even as he did not. His light continued to scan the perimeter.

The cattle dog could not convince him: *No, it's not coyotes.* Her eyes flashed when the beam caught her as she twisted around to bark at the farmer.

Twice she returned and maneuvered

behind the man to urge him forward. He couldn't take more than a few steps before stumbling. Each time she barked, he shouted more harshly, "That'll do!" But she could not stop herself; she was doing what her kind does, what the man had trained her to do. Finally, he swatted her with his long flashlight. She knew it was a warning—he'd never struck her before—but the heavy light slipped from his glove and sunk into the snow ten feet away. She could see the light torpedo through the snow and stall inches above the ground. And that's when the farmer fell silent, turned his back to the cattle dog, and marched toward the farmhouse.

What is the first rule by which a cattle

dog lives? *Where you go, I go.* But this night the heeler knew she would have to finish the work on her own.

After a long time, which was just shy of too long, the drowsing family jerked to attention. There was a sudden snap. Or a clap. Hugging one another, they listened carefully. It was all they could do. If only one of them possessed a cattle dog's ears! Something had cracked the snow—something more than a dog's paws. Yet there was barking—bursts of barking—even if the volume far exceeded anything a dog could produce. It felt as if the earth had cracked along a fault and the widening rift headed directly toward them.

When the father struggled to his feet, the barking's volume increased, but there was nothing to see other than a pale plume of vapor, as if an invisible locomotive were pounding its way toward them.

But instead of a train's blaring horn, a bellowing resounded above the barking and the crunching of ice and the crushing of snow. The father glimpsed a flash of black—that was *not* a wind-flung umbrella. Was it a cow's face? It was. And it wasn't just one cow, but two cows side by side. It was three, four, and then five cows abreast, their rapid breaths clouding the air, their broad chests parting the frozen terrain like icebreakers on a ship's prow. They were a stampede. A bovine thunderstorm. The snow

rumbled and boomed as if some god, suddenly angered, were sending a horrible punishment upon the land.

But then the barking ceased. Then—joltingly—the herd stalled its march as if on command. To the three sets of human eyes, a black cloud—the very squall that had trapped them—had come to rest in the field not twenty yards away from the family's meager bunker. When a cow's ear flicked, there was a flash, briefer than a shooting star, of a yellow ear tag.

Some cows about-faced. Some raised their heads and crooned like plugged tubas. A few separated from the group. But most eyes followed the cattle dog as she veered toward the family.

For a second time, the dog wriggled among

the family's limbs. She wound herself into a circle among their frozen parkas. Her stumpy tail—her whole back end—waggled so hard she almost knocked the boy to the ground. The boy cloaked his arms around her head, and she washed the little of his face that wasn't cloaked with her small, warm tongue. But then she bounded back to the icy surface and barked again, staring at these three lost members of someone's herd. She backed up, barking. She rushed toward the hole again, bowed on her forelegs, and barked. She could not stop until all three humans climbed onto the ice.

The littlest one tried to shimmy across the snow on his belly; he clawed with opposite hands and feet to slide forward. The two larger ones hammered the crust; they trudged and

scraped to grab their way through the snow. Once they were but a few yards from the trench the cattle had plowed, the heeler ceased her barking and her backing-up walk, and trained her entire attention on the cattle. Now, for the third time in a day, her job was to march them, every last one, back to the barnyard.

# Chapter Six

Only when the heeler had marshaled all the
cows into a run ahead of her did the family tread onto the snow corridor the herd had
just plowed and compacted. Where there had
been an impossible impasse of snowfall, there
was now a path almost as wide as the country
roads they had navigated to the lodge.

The sun had set. The herd and the dog
were out of sight even as the family could

hear the rumbling in the distance — yes, it was exactly like sensing an imminent storm. Arms hooked together, unsteady from fear and bone-tired weakness, the family could barely negotiate the uneven channel beneath their boots. They could see the bordering walls of snow in the dim light the shrouded moon granted them. They had to trust that, wherever the cows were headed, it was — at the very least — somewhere.

Beyond exhausted, for her fifth trip across her besieged terrain, the cattle dog could at least run in the path the herd had forged. She found the three people in the middle of the corridor; they were still far from the farmhouse. And they were just sitting on the ground, the small one balled up in the man's arms. She ran straight past the family, turned quickly, and barked at their backs. She pawed the mother's parka. The boy reached over the man's shoulders as if to pet the dog. She growled; he jerked his hand away before she snapped. The heeler rushed in front of the people, jockeyed to either side of them, yapped, and pawed at them until they rose, clinging to one another. The mother slipped and her legs shot out toward the cattle dog. The mother screamed; the dog had only nipped her boot.

To keep them moving, the heeler had to circle them, threaten them with her bared teeth, bark at their scuffling boots. The moment she shot ahead to lead the way they froze in place, forcing her to circle back.

It was only when the barn's yellow light cast

the family's shadows behind them that the cattle dog raced through the broken fence the cows had shattered. She trusted that the people would follow—they had to follow.

After a long time, which was nothing compared to the forever they felt was their future an hour earlier, the family emerged at the lone farmhouse. A huge vapor lamp broadcast its improbable light from under the roof's peak as if the sun had been snagged there on its way up to noon. The light—the first they'd seen since the squall approached—illuminated the snow that frosted the black cows and cast an almost identical shadow of each animal. For an instant, someone might have thought the herd

had doubled in size: the skinniest of the cows flopped onto the ground, while the other half were waiting in the yard for someone to ink in their topmost parts.

Some cows knelt in sleep; some lay on their sides. Some stood, swatted their tails, swayed a bit as if drowsy. Some munched at a long trough between the barn's enormous sliding doors; two roosters skittered among them, pecking at the scattered grain. Big as dinosaur skeletons and bone-white with snow, the baler, skid steer, hay rake, and manure spreader—the blizzard had frozen them in their tracks as well.

# Chapter Seven

The herd's path landed the family at a wide-open gate in a yard surrounded with tubular metal fencing. Inside the corral, the cattle hadn't completely trampled the snow. Dark piles of manure steamed on the white ground. The dog's shallower paw prints wove among the deep hoofprints.

At the far side of the fence, beyond all the cows, feeders, and pens, the family could see that someone had shoveled a long and narrow channel from the barn to the side door of the farmhouse.

Remaining as close to the fence as possible, and moving as quickly as their enervated limbs could carry them, the family concentrated half on where they placed each step, half on what the cows might be doing. Ears flicked. Ears shifted backward and aimed right toward the family to listen. Nostrils flared open to sniff the unfamiliar bodies. With eyes on the sides of their heads, the cattle didn't need to face them to follow their movements.

But it was only as the father began unwrapping the chain that held the gate shut—the jangling links must have signaled something—that all the cows in the yard stirred and swung their heads toward the family in the corner by the padlocked gate.

Two nearby females, their calves in tow, hurried toward them. The four animals were not charging; they did not rake the ground with a hoof, blow steam out their nostrils, lower their horned heads, and break into a run, even though that memory zoomed through the parents' minds. Before the father had spun around to lift the boy over the fence, those four were not ten feet away, and other groups were closing in, striding toward them.

It was the boy who shouted for help.

The snow hadn't been shoveled or trampled on the herd's side of the fence. Ice

glazed the metal rails. Trying to climb, the mother's boots skidded across the slick surface. She tumbled to the snow. The father's gloves slid; he bloodied his nose on the rail.

It was the boy who saw the cattle dog; his parents were facing the farmhouse as they attempted to scale the slick steel rails of the fence. Only the boy saw the single circle the dog ran between his parents and the advancing cows who instantly turned as if the wind in the dog's wake had spun them around.

At the sudden commotion of the retreating cows, the boy's mother and father took one glance over their shoulders. They realized this was their chance: Their eyes locked as if to vow they each could find that last reserve of energy,

but it was panic that catapulted them over the slippery fence and landed them in the shoveled snow beside their son.

# Chapter Eight

Even before someone in the family could explain what had happened, how they had been guided to this place in the middle of nowhere, in the middle of a blizzard, the man who opened the farmhouse door led them to the fireplace. He wedged more logs onto the orange embers. From the closet, he tugged free a stack of nearly identical afghans that someone must have knitted; he draped one and then another around each person. He brought a wet washcloth for the father's blood-smeared face. From the tiny kitchen, he carried out steaming mugs of tea, one at a time.

Then the farmer listened to their teeth chatter as they sipped. When someone started to talk, he held up a hand, as if it were a command: *Wait. It can wait.*

He heated the noodle casserole he'd been eating for dinner that week. He watched their faces turn from pink to white—still a far shade from tan. The boy's eyes could not stay open.

And then the farmer listened to their tale. They had flown to Ohio for a winter vacation. They had been lost—stranded in the blizzard. Out of nowhere, a dog had found them.

She'd warmed them but then ran off into some nowhere from which she'd come. And then she'd driven a herd of cattle—fifty, maybe ninety animals—to flatten the four feet of snow into a path that led them here.

The farmer shook his head.

And then, for the first time since he'd shouted in the barnyard, the boy opened his mouth. He added to the story. The cows suddenly came at them, he said, as if they were going to attack, but when the cows were ready to crush his parents into the fence, the same dog that had rescued them—that very same dog—cut between the cows and his parents and sent the cattle running. She hadn't even barked. And then she disappeared again.

Again, the farmer swiveled his head back and forth. He had a soft voice. He meant to calm the family. Cattle don't just walk over and crush people, he told them. People not knowledgeable about cows might not realize that. And how come all the cows moved toward the family at the gate? The rattling chain? Most often, that means new hay, new buckets of feed.

But to the farmer's ears, their story sounded like a dream. Granted, an awful dream. He did agree that his dog might have smelled their fear at the gate and scattered the barn cows. He did appreciate that they were on the verge of frostbite, of fainting, of shock. They were dehydrated, famished, drained. They had spent most of the day fearing they would never see another day.

But his dog? His cattle? All this had happened . . . even as he'd been right here?

He tugged on his muck boots and jacket, excused himself, and left the family to restore their bodies before the blazing fireplace. He trundled down the shoveled path to the barn.

The cattle dog lay upside down among the square bales stacked on the hay wagon. Her front paws fluttered every now and then. Her muzzle crinkled, her lips lifted, her nose flared. Each inhale filled her nostrils with the scent of her herd—the soured hay called silage, the fresh and dried manure, the cows' grassy breaths. The rhythms of the cows' snorts, grinding jaws, burps, and shuffling hooves

provided the background music that accompanied her sleep. This was her work now: to sleep.

As far as the farmer could tell, the herd appeared to be exactly as he'd left it when the cattle dog roused him hours earlier. Mothers, calves — he didn't count them this time. His flashlight still glowed dimly under the bank of snow.

The strangers' story, despite its desperation, seemed impossible. They had been stranded in that blizzard — perhaps they were delusional. But then, exiting through the open barn doors, the vapor lamp illuminated the herd's pathway through the broken fence — the same section he'd repaired twice this year. The starlight permitted him to see that the corridor continued farther into the pitch dark.

The farmer hesitated. Five, six, seven — the puffs of eight exhales rose and dispersed into the cold air as he stared at his cattle dog, asleep in her favorite position; but then he decided not to whistle and bring her into the house.

How was it the family had managed to leave that farm in Somewhere, Ohio, and never ask the name of the dog?

Maybe if they had seen the dog again. But the three had slept in front of the fire until almost ten the next morning. The farmer had awakened them and towed the family to the lodge in a hay wagon hooked to his tractor.

The sun was almost overhead by the time they arrived; it wasn't such a long distance, but the tractor's plowing blade could only push so much snow ahead of it. The ice shattering beneath those gigantic wheels — it was a sound the boy would never forget. Just as he would never forget the father's desperate whistles, nor the squall's howling, nor the earth cracking open as the herd crashed through the snow.

But the family never saw the farmer's dog again. What might they have said to her? How could three strangers have shown the dog their — their *what?* Gratitude? Love? How could they have repaid it?

Yet it's not thanks for which a dog lives. It's not love — at least, not the kind people need. It's work: The heeler had heard an unfamiliar whistle; she tracked the sound and the smell of something out of place; and she brought the missing back to the farm, because that's a cattle dog's work.

# Epilogue

This is a tale about a cattle dog and a boy. A young cattle dog sleeps between the feet of the boy who is eighteen now and writing this story. The pup had belonged to the farmer whose dog had saved the boy and his parents.

This is how that story ends.

Years after that terrible storm, the boy set off for Ohio the week after high-school graduation. It was early June. Snow was a happily conceded memory in every state he crossed on his route from Florida. He had directions to the lodge. But the farmer's home? He had no idea how many family farms stood in the vicinity of the lodge; the boy had no recollection of where to go.

He knocked on several doors where he saw cattle grazing in lush meadows of alfalfa that had yet to be mowed for the first time that spring. He enlarged his circle around the lodge and continued to search. He remembered the family had walked for hours in the whiteout, but he had no sense of how far they'd traveled.

He started his systematic canvasing again, this time driving onto properties where he saw no cattle at all and nothing to suggest that the right farmer's house lay at the end of this long, curving, gravel driveway—like a pot of gold at the end of a rainbow. (He would never have thought of something so hokey had some child not painted the roadside mailbox to resemble a rainbow.) No, whatever the boy expected to find would not be as in a fantasy or a fairy tale—sudden fortune or immortality. Yet it might hold the ending to an old story he had lived without for nearly half his life.

When the boy wended his way into the backyard of what—amazingly—happened to be the right farmhouse, an elderly man was lobbing a tennis ball across a yard half striped with mounds of fresh clippings that had probably choked the small lawnmower abandoned in the center. A young cattle dog leaped to snatch each toss—almost pirouetting as it zoomed back to deliver the ball. Beside the pasture, knee-high with alfalfa, two cows watched from the nearly empty round-bale feeder in a barn's shadow.

The boy approached. He explained that he was hoping to find the person who had aided his family in the blizzard eight years earlier. The farmer nodded. No one could ever forget that blizzard, he said.

The boy knew that the farmer wouldn't recognize him—even if he did remember the elementary-school kid he had been.

Nor did the boy recognize this man with a walker who ushered him into his farmhouse—which he also didn't recognize.

Nor did he recognize the exuberant, red-ticked cattle dog who joined the man inside, hopping beside him on the couch with a tennis ball fixed in his grin. Nor the fireplace — not right away, not without any firewood or ashes in sight. And then, in an instant, he did: His family had thawed themselves in front of it that night. As imperceptibly as the scent of manure faded from his awareness, the sensation that this *was* the right farm grew stronger.

This *was* the very farm where a dog, a herd of a cattle, and a farmer had saved his family. This *was* the farm in which twenty-four hours shook them from their confident happiness and carefree vacation and made them fragile and mortal again.

So, too, the boy understood that, for the farmer, that particular day was simply one of many on a property where life and death — cows, calves, chickens, turkeys, dogs, rabbits, varmints, people he loved — wrestled for attention most every day.

The boy had posed many questions before another dog he hadn't noticed, asleep on a folded afghan at the base of the stairs, let out a hushed yip that drew his attention.

Yes, the farmer said, that's the dog who rescued your family. Yes, that's Angus, now fifteen, now deaf as a doornail, now blind as a bat — and still — that tired girl is the best cattle dog of the four he had been privileged to work.

And this here is Angus, the farmer explained, stroking the dog who straddled his lap and stared into his eyes. Yes, all four dogs, I named them Angus. They each took up the same place in the barn, in the field, in the house — and in this old heart, that used to be young.

Stories do not always have the ending we imagine they will. The farmer had purchased the cattle-dog pup from the same breeder from which the very first Angus had come. Living in the farmhouse, rather than the barn; watching the farmer train another heeler, rather than work her: The old girl's heart broke.

Then a month after he got the pup, the farmer's best producing, *least* unpredictable cow kicked her rear hooves squarely onto the farmer's backside and shattered his pelvis. Broke it in four places. He managed one phone call before he fell unconscious.

It is true, the farmer had intentionally shrunk his herd over the years. He kept fewer calves. He didn't really have the drive to put up with keeping a bull on his farm for once-a-year breeding and pretty much year-round problems. Since his wife died—would have been three years before that blizzard—all farming really needed to do was keep him busy, keep him company.

From the hospital bed in Columbus, he called the Wheelers, who ran the livestock auction, and told them to head over and take all but the two oldest cows. It wasn't their normal practice to pick up animals, but after close to fifty years of selling his cows, the farmer figured one favor wasn't much to ask of them.

He also figured this little accident was going to cost a pretty penny, starting with the helicopter ride — first he'd ever taken. Heck, he wouldn't even have known he'd taken it, except he awakened briefly, foggily, as the orderlies transferred him from the ER gurney to his hospital bed and said the words "life flight."

At the hospital, even though the specialist (a woman! Now that surprised the farmer as well) said his bones would heal on their own without surgery, he'd be looking at three months of lying low. A nurse would check in on him. Someone would come three times a week and help him regain some strength and stability. All that was going to add up. No sense being all proud and then falling—that would just make the recovery worse.

The new heeler, he admitted, had been a mistake. A mistake the farmer didn't imagine making. The pup had no work to do on the farm now, and deserved a far better life than the farmer could offer. First six weeks after the accident, the only exercise the heeler got was the farmer tossing a tennis ball down the basement steps. The dog's feet would hit the first few steps, but then he'd leap from midstairs to the bottom, scramble around to find the ball among all the farmer's late wife's whatnots and the stuff his two kids expected they might want someday, bound up the stairs, his feet hitting all the steps this time, and put the ball in the man's hand. It got to be that, in the instant it took for the farmer to reach back and toss again, the dog would already be stationed at the bottom of the stairs, all four legs cocked and ready to spring in one direction or the other, poised for the catch.

There came a longer pause in the farmer's talking when the boy thought he might change the subject without exactly interrupting. He wanted to know something — anything, really — about the cattle dog's training. Specifically, he wondered what the farmer might have taught the old Angus so that she could have known how to find his family? What made her drive the cows to them? Did she know that they would trample a path that the people could use?

The farmer had a lot to share about the heelers' heritage — why, they're bred from Australian dingoes! — and their herding instincts and their tireless determination. He explained about reward training, and how you have to keep sessions short and always successful. He said how you need a long lead on the collar and an even longer amount of patience to let out. But he had none of the answers the boy had hoped to hear.

After another pause, the boy asked if he could go out to the barn and the corral. He wanted to see if his childhood recollections were exaggerated. He didn't think so, but some people who had heard his tale looked doubtful. The boy wanted to know how far the dog had driven the cattle that night in the blizzard. How tall was the steel gate they had to climb to escape the cows that night? Is the same tractor there—the one with the enormous wheels?

The farmer pointed toward the door that opened onto the walkway to the corral and he told the boy to go on, have your eyeful of the place, and come inside for sandwiches afterward—unless, of course, you need to head back by a certain time.

The boy pulled open the back door.

The red-ticked heeler pushed through the unlatched screen door with his muzzle and sprinted toward the barn as if he knew the very answers this boy wanted and had every intention of showing the boy now — and later and as long after that as the stranger could stay.

The boy rapped on the screen door. He could see two TV trays with sandwiches and glasses of milk set in front of the couch where the farmer snored softly. He entered the farmhouse quietly. The old Angus still dozed by the stairs. The young Angus — he'd found a squirrel to pursue and left the boy as he veered toward the back porch.

The boy dropped to his knees and gradually crawled toward the sleeping dog. He didn't want to startle her. He didn't want her to wake. Even if she could hear or see, the dog couldn't have perceived the boy as anything but a stranger — albeit, a different one than he'd been eight years ago. He sidled close to the dog's body — watching for any sign that she might awaken — until the arch of her bony, silver-black body pressed against his chest and the tops of his thighs. This time, the warmth of the tears that slid onto the dog's fur did not surprise him.

His top arm cinched the dog's chest and his hand pressed the rising and falling V below her rib cage as if to cup each slow, labored breath. He matched his breathing to hers. Whatever shape he had supposed his belated, speechless gratitude might have taken,

this was it. Here was the dog to whom he owed his life. A dog with the name of Angus. Angus the third. And the farm and the dogs—they would continue without her. Her work there was done.

When the farmer's walker rattled one of the TV trays, the boy gently unwrapped himself from the dog and returned to the chair facing the fireplace, as if he, too, had simply needed a nap. The old Angus continued to dream on her afghan that, yes, the boy remembered: It had wrapped his own body that night. The new Angus pawed at the screen door. The farmer told the pup to go find something to chase and leave the grown-ups to talk a minute. Indeed, as if the earlier conversation had been a dream, upon waking, the farmer wanted to ask the questions now. So where in Florida you live? Why come to this part of Ohio? What now, after high school? Were his parents well?

The two-year-old, red-ticked cattle dog who sleeps between the feet of the boy as he finishes this story belonged to the farmer. He may be Angus the fourth, but the only name that calls him is Rescue.

The boy, who is now the sole member of the cattle dog's herd, did not find all the answers to the questions that sent him back to Ohio. For all he learned from the farmer, he did not find a real ending to this story. Instead,

he found, as every cattle dog finds every day, that answers and endings are, in truth, just beginnings trying to be patient. That there is always work to do.